WRITER'S BLOCK

STORIES FROM THE LITTLE BLACK NOTEBOOK

MICHAEL STICCO

authorHOUSE®

AuthorHouse™
1663 Liberty Drive
Bloomington, IN 47403
www.authorhouse.com
Phone: 833-262-8899

Published by AuthorHouse 12/16/2020

ISBN: 978-1-6655-1133-9 (sc)
ISBN: 978-1-6655-1132-2 (e)

Print information available on the last page.

This book is printed on acid-free paper.

CONTENTS

PREFACE

"You are not Dostoevsky,' said the woman …
'You never can tell … ' he answered.
'Dostoevsky is dead,' the woman said, a bit uncertainly.
'I protest!' he said with heat, 'Dostoevsky is immortal!"
Mikhail Bulgakhov from *Master and Margarita*

Stories are what drive humanity to convey complex thoughts and emotions to one another. My intention behind the content in this book is neither radical nor traditional in the way in which I grew up to understand such a word. These are not the stories of man's fall into madness or the triumph of good over evil: it is a personal analysis and show of the transition from a young author to a still young, but slightly older author. The slow transition of a young person's life and the meaning of their ever changing influences. A collection of work between the winter of 2014 to the Spring of 2020. These works have seen anywhere between a year to six years of edits and revisions set in the backdrop of the transition period between an aspiring teenager to someone who resembles an adult on his own in the world.

Like most writing, the beginning is stranger than the fiction written on the page. For that reason at the end of each story, I lay out my thoughts about the story's influence and why it was chosen from a fairly large file of other ramblings and into this book. They are not answers to any questions, but simply my thoughts about them as works to be elaborated on since there may be some embedded confusion based on the fact that no one knows everything. As any beginning would have it, I chose a quote from one of my personal favorite authors, Mikhail Bulgakhov from his best known work, The Master and Margarita. A book I read in college whose story behind the book is more meaningful to me than the actual book itself. A Russian Author whose stories revealed life beyond the scope of what a single person can experience in a lifetime. That is the influence that is captured here in these pages. None of us are Dostoyevsky, Bulgakhov, Orwell, Shelley, Rowling, Speilberg, nor Burnham: Yet through their influence, you can never really know that beyond a reasonable doubt.

The best hope I can possibly have for my little creature is that it influences at least one person to create a response. That is where I end my introduction, on a Chekhov quote. An author who, to me, always enjoyed the last word in a conversation.

"The role of the artist is to ask questions, not answer them."

Anton Chekhov

The Smoker's Tale

"Wanna hit?" She lifted the small chode of a blunt to meet my sight. The moonlight was bright and lit her hair, but her face was lit by the burning fire which lay far behind me. I took another puff of my cigarette. Even without the help of the cigarette, we could see the air move with the exhalations that carried our breath up into the sky.

I reached for the blunt with my other hand and brought it to my mouth, but as I took a deep inhale, I remembered my piss test was coming in two weeks. Still, I didn't let that bother me. I knew I needed this. I felt like a weight had been lifted from my head, and for a brief second I thought life was worth its struggle. I held the smoke in until I could feel the warm tingle crawl to every inch of my chest. Then exhaled.

The fields of unborn crops, the dirt- and rock-laden road that divided the fields into neat and portioned pieces, and the corner we stood at were all lit by this hue of grey and blue. The road even took on this color, but in the distance, as it ran past me and into the foreground, it started to take to the luminescence of the fire and show the part that was all dirt.

I looked back to see what this fire was. "Isn't that the McAllen farm house?" I handed the blunt back to her.

A rough outline of a two-story building stood entangled in tall flames that danced a sacrificial rhythm, entirely consumed with the fire. I wondered if it had softened the tundra on the field. I dug my heel into the ground to test it. My heel struck the ground to break off a couple chunks of loose dirt, cemented by the cold.

"It *was* their farm house." I paused to look back at the intersection of the road a short distance away. The light of the moon may have illuminated most of the fields, but its light could not reach the darkness of the edge of the woods. I took a puff of my cigarette, and at that moment I felt like running over there. It seemed so safe; the fantasy of leaving felt like a new taste of freedom. "They moved away years ago. Where to?" Her face seemed to shrug as if to say *I don't know.*

Her eyes moved on the ground, but even though she wasn't looking at the fire, I could still see the glow of the flames reflecting off her eyes, to the point that I could not recognize what her natural eye color was.

I took another deep draw of my cigarette. Finally my nerves had calmed down to where I realized my toes had stopped twitching. "Then who was in the house?"

A white car approached the corner, turned, and raced toward the fire. Its red and blue lights came on, and the white car turned into a haze of red and blue as it kicked up dirt and mud behind it.

"Let's head back," I took another puff of the cigarette. She tossed out her blunt and started to walk toward the fire. I kept my cigarette, took another puff, and started to walk behind her.

Author's Note

I woke in the middle of the night in my eight by eight single dorm room, a few hours before my alarm would go off. I knew I had to take out my laptop and start fiercely writing down everything I remembered from the dream I just had. This story is everything I remembered from that dream, written from my point of view in the rawest form I could. It remains a mystery to me who this other person was, why we were there on the corner, and who started the fire. If my friend and I started the fire, then why go back? If not, then what were we doing there in the first place?

While editing it for the first time in two years, I realized those weren't the questions I should be asking. I thought about the symbolism of the fire surrounding a cold night—a reoccuring theme I like to try an insert. Where night is typically something to fear, I always found comfort in the rural country roads under the moonlight. When the moon is out, there is nothing to be afraid of, and I tried to convey that in the calm demeanor of the characters.

THE CLASS

He sits in one of those little chairs that have the little desktop that can barely hold a sheet of paper and a pencil. He's trying to pay attention to the words that his professor vomits profusely from his mouth at the front of the class. The key word is "trying," as the reality of the situation is that our protagonist is currently gawking into the black line that separates the two white boards, dreaming of the day he'll leave university and live in the real world. The freedom and liberty to read what he wants to read and the freedom to write in the forms and papers he feels passionate about, instead of whatever generic form he's being forced to pay half his attention to. At least the professor is passionate about his subject and isn't dull. The word *Bueller* comes to mind in the repetitive monotone we've come to attribute to dull teachers.

The student's name is Jon, and he's a regular university student with the aspiration of becoming something big. Exactly what that might be is still a mystery to both him and myself. However, Jon likes to daydream, and while his professors preach as though they were messiahs to their areas of knowledge, Jon doesn't care. On this day, Jon stares at that black line in the front of the class for what feels to be hours on end. The black line turns to the line of a railing to a ship. Jon approaches the railing to see the night lights of a sea shore city.

"Hey, boss." An annoyingly high male voice reaches out of the darkness of the ship. "We got the shipment, but what are we doing here with it anyway? You know the party won't allow this stuff to be brought in!"

"The Soviets will pay anything, any bribe, to receive this good shipment," Jon said in a slick tone. He's dressed in a trench coat dreaming of being a Russian mafioso. He's delivering a shipment of handcrafted Italian purses into the city of Odessa. *All for the money*, Jon tells himself as he creates the next part of his daydreaming.

The thrill and the excitement builds in him: will he be busted by the Soviets, or will everything go according to plan?

"That's all for class today. Read pages 141 to 145 in your textbook, and do exercises three to six in your activities manual."

Jon is sucked back into reality. Just as easily as the vision had come, it was gone and forgotten as he stuffed his laptop into his backpack, slung it over his shoulder, and left the room as quickly as possible.

Jon goes to the cafeteria where he sits down, plugs in his music, and gets ready for the next class. A fascinating class with a monotone teacher, another victim fallen to the Mondays. A disease in the face of society, but really it's his fault for picking such a terrible class, Medieval Latin Literature in Translation. A bunch of dead writers, who wrote in a now-dead language, translated by dead people all about people who don't matter or relate to anyone's life or culture. They aren't even written by people who experience life, just monks! The medieval geeks who hid from the giant gaseous ball in the sky to write of those who don't.

Author's Note

My apologies to my professor of Russian literature in college, but I confess that there were times I would let my mind drift in class. However, I completely blame the authors for being engaging enough to merit a response in the literary sense and not my obviously short attention span. Like another work in this book, I drafted this in the middle of class—quite literally wrote in class about daydreaming in class about the class material. Yet I offer this story more as an homage to the teachers and professors who enjoyed teaching the material so much that it infected my brain to the point where I found myself distracted by the material and thirsty for more than the time they were allotted. It is destructive in the short term and makes me a poor student, but I always enjoyed showing my teachers that the sweat and labor they went through did have an effect on at least one student, and I was fortunate to have several of these, specifically my French, English, and Russian professors.

This story illustrates that it is how the teacher can influence the way the student perceives what is taught. Yeah, Jon doesn't care about what the professor is saying, but he is still taking in every word within his daydream. There is something supernatural about the power of words and how someone uses them.

GIRL IN THE NIGHT

They hung around the tables and chairs and onto each other in their drunken manner. I remain seated and watch the time walk around the sea of drunken toddlers. The air ran mad with the incense of sex, booze, and tobac. This asylum of the freed who ran wild barked their proclamations into the night. The cold fizzle of my cola was a foreigner amidst the waves of cocktails. My sober clarity stood alone in that crowd. My chair was situated up to the dining room table which was temporarily modified to a drinking games table so I could watch these games for entertainment. Then among the crowd she came through the threshold like a summer's breeze through a window. She floated in as though she were a ghost. The world was unobservant to her mysterious grace and long flowing hair. Her deep distinct features lightly outlined her face under the poor light of the room and grew as she sat. Her eyes stared back into mine and back down, as though she was trying to keep me out, making me feel as though I were staring at a wall, a stone cold wall. Under the dim light, her black pants matched a perfect black to her shirt. Her shirt, though, fit more like a short dress that went to her hips than a shirt, but not enough to be a blouse. I would never know. Her shirt was obviously transparent and her tank top made up for its transparency so to the average drunk, it all looked like a single top. Her skin painted a ghostly image and left me to wonder if she was actually in front of me. She just sat there watching closely to the games being played in front of her, in front of me. Her hair ran smooth, falling down her head like a shiny mocha waterfall hiding her soft face in the curtain of those falls. Her hair sat over her shoulders so her face appeared a lost paradise in the middle of a jungle. The jungle walls hid her from the world, untouched by the evils of man. Her eyes lifted to meet my own and stayed this time. Those grey eyes stared so comfortably into mine. Maybe they're inviting, but I didn't know. Should I run, screaming and shouting, away? Or should I stay in this time lock with her, at this place, in this dark endless night. Her eyes turned into the stars in the sky and the feeling of the cool night air in your face rushed to my head.

My heart sank deep into my chest. I got up and walked around the table to grab her hand. She then met my hand and ran with me. Her mystery left me in wonder as time slowed, but gravity was slower as I dropped my drink, yet she moved quicker. I could have sworn we left the room before the drink hit the floor. She glided across and over the drunken crowd as I crashed into every last person. Time sped up as we neared the door. Her warm hand guided my freezing one, an unbreakable connection, a line darted to the door into the cold night. Even when we were outside, alone and safe, we kept running through the blackwall of the night. We ran so far the lights of the house disappeared and nothing was left. I caught up and we were running into nothing. All of my previous thoughts of what was beyond that lighted prison was false. I found the moonlit fields rather than an abyss. I found woods where I thought there was a hole. I found a home where I had thought there was a frozen hell. The night was cold yet inviting; a distinct difference I learned between cold and frozen. A thought I'd never believed to think of. She stopped and we sat in the field of dirt, a plot on a hill between two forests and overlooking a lake. The moon revealed everything in the field and just over the tree line to our night was the illumination of that timed asylum.

The lake itself was like a supernatural being all on its own. How large it was, if we looked left or right, it would go on for miles. We looked across and the other shore looked too far to swim, but the stars clearly showed the rolling hills on the other end, illuminated in a wash in that natural nightlight. A few scattered trees on the coast line, but all fields up the hills. The water was calm as it seemed there was no life existing in the lake at that time. I felt as though the night took my hand to show me this magnificent sight.

We looked up and there were those stars and purple swirls of the galaxy. So naked and bare the night was, as I looked over to see her eye closed. She sat down, head tilted back, and I laid down observing how the moon shined her hair to resemble the night sky. Her hands supported her from behind and her eyes remained shut to everything. I sat up and she opened her eyes. They were now black like the wall. She sat up only to rest her light, soft head on my chest as I held her for her support.

I said in a low sincere voice "Let me in the wall you've built around yourself so we burn it down."

She remained unaltered by my words. She finally raised

her head, with soft tears rolling down curves of her face in a glimmering line of pain, "So then what? We dance around the ash?" She wept. She threw her head back onto my chest and held each other for a small spot of warmth in the cold night.

The night may never end, but the time she died was a moment no one wept, for tears were emotions those bastards never felt. I knew her and she knew me. In our short time in purgatory together, she numbed the pain and breathed warm air into a cold night.

I don't want to live forever, not with some light-hearted fool's escape. The harsh realities of the world. She was real, in here with me, now I am alone. If I close my eyes, it felt like nothing had changed and it hurt. To them, I'm transparent as a ghost. I'm haunted to keep running farther and endless so I keep running. Today's the day I wept for her, the first time since and her pain feels the same, but night continued, the cold remained cold and to dust, we all shall return.

Author's Note

This is the oldest of all the works here and is the first novella written back in the winter of 2014. First and foremost, this was partly influenced by a dream I had that grew into a short story about a short lasting love. In the year leading up to this, I had gotten over my first real breakup as a teenager, found myself more, started a new relationship, and felt confident enough to pour my heart and soul into writing. The conversation is edited lyrics from one of my favorite songs at the time, *Dust To Dust* by the Civil Wars because it matched with the dream and mood of the whole story.

I showed the earliest draft to a friend who asked, "okay but who is the girl?" I did not have a response for her because the girl wasn't meant to be anyone, I initially thought. Then, I thought she was my ex, my new love interest, or even a combination of different people. However now, she was not any of them, but rather the missing piece to the main character. Someone who everyone wishes to be with in their own way. But that's my answer to my own question, a subjective view really. Chekhov would frown at me for this note.

Just like in *The Smoker's Tale*, the darkness is a comforting place away from the distractions and soulless motions I felt like I would go through sometimes in high school, college, and even now. Rather night here is a bubbled world away from the one we know and can feel endless but in a way that makes the characters feel more connected to the more meaningful things in life.

DEAR ANNA

I

"Dear Anna,

*I'm sorry if I don't make any sense, but I'm writing late at night and I must let you know that **I no longer love** you."*

[Voicemail April 9th, 2014]

Hey mom, sorry it's so late, I just got home from that date. He picked me up and we went to a nice little restaurant in the city, talked about his job and how he met you and when you decided you needed to show him my picture. You never told me he had worked with you at the office for so long, apparently you guys don't work on the same floor, so that explains why you never met him before. But either way, after a nice little dinner, we went to the MET to look at the paintings. We laughed at some of the paintings, made up little stories like how I used to do as a kid. It was going great, until we saw some paintings by Jacque-Louis David and Marie-Denise Viller. He stood there a while in a very uncomfortable silence, but after his attitude completely changed from happy to something that made me feel very melancholy. I don't think we'll be going back out. It looks like he might be going through something, let me know if you know anything. Love you, talk to you in the morning! [Beep]

II

*"Our time together felt so short and it was meaningful and blissful, yet even then it was nothing more than **a facade**."*

[February 25ᵗʰ, 2013]
From: Killian.Kratz@Mail.com
Subject: You Okay?

Finn,

You doing alright over there bro, it's been weeks since any of us have seen or heard from you? We've tried texting, calling, but none of us have been able to get a hold of you. I know you're still working from home, so you're using email, just give me a reply or a call, I think we should meet up.

[February 27ᵗʰ, 2013]
From Finnian.McFay@Mail.com
Subject: re:You Okay?

Killian,
Yeah sorry, I've been trying to delve into my work to distract myself. I had to ditch my phone, the phone and

cable bills were getting too much with everything else happening. Let the guys know I'm doing alright, wana go to our pub on 8ᵗʰ Ave this saturday? I think some human interaction should be good.

✂

[February 27ᵗʰ, 2013]
From Killian.Kratz@Mail.com
Subject: re:re:You Okay?

Yeah sounds good, I'll grab the guys and see you then.

✂

[March 3ʳᵈ, 2013]
From Killian.Kratz@mail.com
Subject: re:re:re:You Okay?

Finn,

Nice to see you're doing better, thanks for coming out buddy. Now get a damn phone! I'm sick of having to email you to get your attention! Like you said, the hospital bills are almost over with so give me a text or else I'll get your mother involved! Haha see you around bro.

P.S. When you can, bring Charlotte over, the missus has been asking about her like crazy!

III

*"In the moment you meant everything to me. I regret to say that you still do. Dammit, now **I'm a liar and alone**. What did this all mean to you if it was for nothing?"*

Mom,   November 13th, 2012

Dr. Felser said I need to write to everyone who helped me to find help, but you're the only person who was there and literally dragged me here. I have to admit this has been a very trialing experience for me, but after four months I'm glad you got me here. I've been eating and drinking again; the Doctors said I'll be okay so long as I have something to focus on, which when I get out will be a new job in the city I've been probing for about a week now. Just can't tell them I'm in the loony bin, at least I'll be able to hide it as a regular hospital visit if they ask. However for now I've taken up painting, which is nice since they have the internet here; I'll send a painting next on my reply, I'm in the middle of a very good portrait right now. But I'm enjoying the neoclassical french painters!

I've also achieved to be able to talk about Anna a little bit. It seems the best mindset to have is focusing on getting better which means I'll be able to leave soon. To be honest I still really hurt. There's a pit in my stomach just thinking about it and eating usually doesn't make it better, so a coping mechanism has been to paint all night and continue. Let me know how home is and please send pictures, I'm not sure how much longer I'll be here for before the doctor says I'm alright, and I'd like to see some of you, dad, and Charlotte while I'm here.

Love you!
Your favorite (and only) son

IV

*"Loneliness frightens me; when you were here, it didn't exist in that space of time, but now it consumes me. I want to blame someone or something for this, but all I can do is cry on **the impression you left** on our bed."*

My Dear Finn; my love,   August 19th, 2012

Please forgive me, but I'm tired. I've been tired of living day to day with the weight of the baggage over my head for my entire life now. It never subsides; always relentless, and when there is a hint that it is subsiding, I worry about the next time it arrives and then it does. I cannot help but to notice it lingering on and on. You know how much of a fight it was while we were dating, you tried your best to understand and help me; but I never had the heart to tell you that there was nothing you could do to relieve me of this torture. I'm sorry for lying to you about that. I don't want to leave bed because I'm afraid of disappointing you, I'm afraid of hurting the child I'm carrying. I'm afraid of what she'll turn out to become and if my anxiety will be onto her! I've thought about this for a while now and the more I push it off the worse it gets for me. I don't want to do this and leave you to be a single father. I've arranged everything to go to you so you can move forward. Please, when I'm gone forget about me. I beg you to not think about me and not be in pain because of me. I'm not meant to be here, nor was I ever meant to. I love you with all my heart, now it's time to finally rest well. I love you.

-With deep sorrow and love, your Anna

V

"I'm sorry I couldn't save you; I couldn't breath life back into your heart, but lying to myself is the only way I can move forward with my life. I want to know where I can go when you're not around anymore and I'm feeling down.
*-With **deep love and sorrow**, your Finn*
January 1ˢᵗ, 2014"

[A Note Left on the Tombstone of Anna McFay on April 9th, 2018]

It's been five years and nine months since you left us. Five long, painful years. This is the first time I've been able to see you since your funeral. It was a beautiful day, I hope you got to see the sunset like we used to do. I love you still, even after grieving for so long.

Things got a lot easier now that Charlotte is home. I used to look at her, see your face, and run away. She lived with you mother then mine for a short period of time and it's only been since the summer of 2014 that she's been with me, for which I'm extremely grateful for. She has your light blue eyes, curly strawberry blonde hair, and soft turn-up nose; it kind of breaks my heart to see such things. A little over a year in the hospital we were able to celebrate her second birthday at home. I'm also grateful both our mothers are so passionate about this little girl. She brings such joy into my life; heck she brings joy everywhere she goes, hence her middle name, Charlotte Anna McFay, after the woman who brought so much joy to my life. We miss you and I've started to show her pictures of you. She thinks you're "the most beautiful woman in the whole wide world" and I'm forced to agree. Although she took your knack to writing, so I'm waiting for the diaries to pile up. She especially loves to write little notes on my paintings, almost like poems if I say so, you mother has been calling them "collaborations" and I loved it.

In the meantime I've managed to find a job with a fancy company and been promoted to head of finances, which means I finally bought that cabin we had our eyes on for years, Charlotte loves it so much. We'll be having 4th of July there this year with the whole family. Next time I'll bring Charlotte and she can give you one of our collaboration projects.

Love you forever,
Finn and Charlotte

Author's Note

I started writing this in a creative writing course during college, while I intentionally put in the effort to ignore what my teacher was saying purely out of spite for the way he taught the material. Yet he did manage to influence the mood of the story quite a bit. I always complained that the material he used had the same attitude, life is short, you will be miserable no matter what you do, you will die, and you will die alone. I don't understand how you can find so many sad stories to fill a semester of teaching. He might have been a literary sadist, which also doesn't make sense because he would always tell us about how excited he was for his wedding coming up and wanted us to send him song requests that he could play at the wedding. A happy guy, but really enjoyed the saddest stories. We read Emily Dickinson and that was probably the happiest author we read.

Regardless, This professor's influence started this story with the words, " I must let you know that I no longer love you" and suddenly I knew I wanted to dig deeper. This story is more about the trip to revealing information in a parallel way, like a road, how one side goes one way, and the other side moves the other direction. The italicized words make up one letter that slowly reveals more as the story progresses. The body uses different mediums (voicemail, email, and letters) to build a backwards timeline of events, first indirectly the building to the personal aspect. A literal timeline as it was important that all the messages and letters had dates attached to them. All of this cultivates to the very last letter which caused a lot of internal struggle. Initially it was supposed to end with Finn killing himself too in some Romeo and Juliette fashion, but I realized that would not be a satisfying ending. That is why the decision to do the opposite was written in and to me and my housemate who read the first draft, made the story more compelling and emotional.

The exercise in this is that through edits, the story starts as a mystery, then slowly questions are answered as you learn more about the characters. It builds until you know Finn and Anna's history, then it concludes on a note that all those stories in my writing composition class lacked; creation.

MORNING

My thoughts remain long and exhausting, yet not enough to relieve me of my sufferings. On my bed I toss and turn through the night, while I'm never completely in my bed. Alone, it seems that the morning may be my enemy, as I grasp for the night to restart so I might rest my mind. At night the world rests; the people, the animals, even the weather conduct their unconscious ritual and remain undisturbed. To betray this ritual, my mind becomes my inquisitor. But there's nothing that compares to the sound of the first bird chirping early in the morning. To have your long stride of restlessness, the bird's chirp is the closest thing to a friend from a long and lonely night. It comes up as a surprise for the night watch, but a surprise friend is better than no friend.

Artificial thoughts are nice for the learning aspirer. "Remain calm, breathe, and relax" templated in your mind. Yet, upon this restless night, my mind was tormented by all the unfinished tasks and all the unsaid words I never uttered. It would seem the only ones who don't have these issues are the dew birds, whom I grow to envy and despise.

Dominion within the back of my mind, it is these unsaid words which have plagued the words and stretched fully across vast lands and thrashed at the soul of this damned man. Words are nothing that concerns the dew bird, but rather us who all are under their spells that they cast as harmonious choir every morning of every day for a millenia.

It is those words, regretfully never said, that seem to have defined how a person becomes as opposed to who they become. The bird's chirp is a constant reminder of the nostalgia that remains in the absence of the person. A reminder that time has marched on and who that person can never be. The rémanence of a blue sky in the early morning sky, how its' hue terrorizes on the psyche of our eternal trip to seeming purgatory.

Still, the question remains of who was wrong and who was right? How many words remained trapped in the labyrinth of mind who could have been freed into the conversation. The fault is long placed on one person to scare their silhouette in our minds. Yet these excuses will remain to only taint the image that is so desired.

Others try to take the crown of victory, only for memories to win against the struggle. Again the only reminder of these memories, words and lack thereof are those damned birds which haunt me in my restlessness as they sing their songs and ballads.

Never has there been, in such a lifetime, such a haunting as your ghost does onto my restless soul. It's by these dew birds, that I am haunted, the morning hue of blue everywhere always finds a way to keep me awake through the early morning hours. It is for this, that I try not surrender myself to the alliance my mind has made with you. Then a new letter will need to be written and another mind will be wasted at night. Damn those dew birds in their beauty.

Author's Note

Morning started as Mindless Ramblings From A Sleep Deprived Madman. It was the early morning when I started to write this, just as the birds began to wake up. I had another sleepless night in my dorm, one of many. However, the night really gave the time to compose each line deliberately and on the other end I had to lose quite a bit of sleep because I edited this line by line. Therefore this story is meant to be read line by line just as in poetry.

This story was ironically influenced by a poem I wrote years ago, only tainted by nostalgia;

> *"There's this memory I have on a winter's day,*
> *In the early morning she woke up,*
> *And stared at the beauty of the fresh layer of snow outside.*
> *I don't remember the snow, but I remember her."*
>
> *-2017*

This story and poem comes from a very personal place in my heart and I included it as an exercise in deliberately writing each line as though everything had meaning while none of it mattered. That something pleasant at first can turn bitter with time. As the birds are admired at first, they are resented by the end; and sometimes we need a good night's sleep more than anything else.

CHEAP THRILL

He rushed over to the freezer to take out the frozen peas that he was supposed to thaw before he put the pasta in the boiling water. He wiped the sweat from his forehead, placed the peas under the hot water, and he slid over to the pasta cooking behind him. The sauce had been done for a while and sat on a low burn as he realized he had poorly planned the timing for the food for this date.

Bzz Bzz, his phone vibrated. It was her.

Idk, ummm how about 9? The text message read. He looked at the clock that read eight.

SHIT! He thought to himself. He replied, *Yeah that works, just finishing up dinner. Then I'll change and will pick you up.*

That was all a lie. The plan was to cook dinner so they could dress up all nice and eat as the sun set. He had it all planned, but none of it was finished except for the sauce. On top of that, he still had not showered!

Then he checked the pasta impulsively for the next ten minutes until it was cooked; then set the burner to low, ripped off his pants, and jumped into the shower.

Ok so if I got in the shower at 8:12 and take a 5-minute shower (8:17), he put on body wash, *get dressed in the tux ...*

tie the bow tie … but I don't think I have a bow tie … Shit I have to go with a tux. He then applied shampoo, *SHIT I forgot to set the place.* He put on the conditioner, rinsed it then jumped out of the shower. *So I'll run out in shorts to finish placing the table and leave to pick her up at 8:30, so long as I'm in the car no later than 8:25.* It was already 8:17.

He ran as fast as he could outside in nothing but his underwear, placed the table in the location he had planned earlier that day. He grabbed place mats and a cover, and put those to use to decorate the outdoor table into a romantic place setting, or the best he could do with two minutes to spare.

He ran inside and threw on his tux, and fiddled with the bowtie until he realized it was already 8:30! *SHIT! I'm going to be late!* He prayed for a miracle and finally was able to tie his bowtie in a manner that was acceptable for such a rush. He opened the peas, put them in a bowl, threw them in the microwave, and ran off to his car.

When he checked the time, it was 8:34. He looked at himself in the rear view mirror and saw the reflection of a clean man in a cheap tux. He complimented himself, *Man, I clean up pretty well for not having done anything a half an hour ago.* Only he was able to lie so well to himself, that he knew there'd be something he'd missed and would be made fun of for it.

On the contrary, She had been ready for this night and was sitting in her robe in her room. She waited peacefully for 8:40 to come so she could put on the red dress that she was asked to wear for the night. She was excited that she was finally able to wear it and he knew it, especially since he was there when she picked it out; She debated buying such a dress with no immediate occasion to wear it, but he knew she loved the dress, so he made up an excuse. Hence why he set up such a cliché date night. A 'formal' dinner, in a not so formal place.

She slipped on the red dress and went back into the bathroom to see what make-up she should touch up on. Her little sister stomped into the bathroom, "That's the most make-up I've ever seen you wear," the little sister said. She had never really worn too much make-up to begin with, so to wear foundation, some blush, and red lipstick was a lot of make-up for her.

"You know I have date night tonight, right?" The attitude in her voice rose toward her younger sibling.

"I don't know," the younger sibling complained, "I don't try to keep up with your life." Then left the room.

Bzz Bzz, She opened the text message from him, *Here.* More romantic words could not have been spoken from Romeo himself, toward his young Juliette.

Shit, she thought, I'm not ready yet.

He greeted her at the door and kissed her cheek. He took her to his old beat up jeep and opened the door for her as though it were her chariot. He sat in the driver's seat and pulled out of her driveway in the old clanker. *Such an interesting sight to see, two well-dressed people, who look like they're off to a fancy dinner at some 5-star hotel dinner, but nope they're having pasta and peas in a backyard, only a couple yards away from a lake with smelly fish,* he thought. Regardless, she was happy that she could wear her new red dress and he was happy to make her happy.

When they arrived at his house, She gasped, "It's beautiful." A single candle was lit at the centerpiece; he guided her to the table, pulled out her chair, then proceeded to ask her if she would like anything else. She shook her head to say no with a smile so big, he felt compelled to kiss her dimpled cheek. She had never been treated like this before, but always wanted to do such a thing.

He rushed inside and placed all the food in near and fair portions on the plates then brought out two plates and set them on the table before realizing he forgot the drinks. "water please," she still wore that smile with sheer euphoria.

The golden rays of the sun stretched to highlight her face as she ate the pasta and he was amazed. She looked up, "I'm actually getting a little cold." He got up, took off the jacket of his tux, and proceeded to place it on her shoulders. She felt warm again and somehow smiled even more than before. She looked at him in his white tuxedo shirt, red bowtie, and red cumber button. "Thank you," She said and continued to eat.

After they finished dinner, he put the plates and silverware in the kitchen, blew out the candle, and took her back in his car. She was confused as this was not part of the plan he told her originally. He took her to the beach on the lake. She kicked her shoes off to walk barefoot on the sand in her red dress.

The sun laid just below the horizon at this point and the first stars appeared in the sky. They both walked barefoot in the sand. He pulled up his pants to his knees, looking ridiculous as he could, she laughed. He walked into the water up until it went to his pants. He extended his hand to her. She looked at him and thought to herself, *I'm not getting my dress wet*, but then she found herself picking up the bottom of her dress to meet his hand in the water.

They stood hand in hand. They looked at the magnificent view together; she, toward the phenomenon of the setting sun and rising stars; and he, toward her face, trying his best to memorize every last detail from her wild hair line, to her brown eyes, down the bumps of her cheek created by the foundation of her make up, and finishing at the small bump on the bottom of her face, She called a chin, but he called *The Bump*.

Later they wound up back in the car and drove with the moon to their backs. They had lost track of time and how long they watched the sun go over the horizon, but that time had become irrelevant, and it was okay. It was date night, some cheap thrill. In the car, they talked about the current gossip going on in their lives and what they were doing for the better part of the year while separated. Eventually they arrived back at his house.

They went up to his room, turned on the television and put on her favorite show. She put on her favorite shorts and hoodie that she always likes to steal when she comes over, he only wore shorts as pajamas, and they crawled into bed. Scattered articles of fine clothing thrown into one pile on the floor, like a small hill. He laid on his back as she laid with her head resting on his chest. Her top leg hurdled over his body as the other laid down with his legs. His arm wrapped around her enough to play with her hair which she loved to have her hair played with and he loved to play with it. She fell asleep thinking of how wonderful the night was and how exhausted she was even though they had barely done anything that day.

Yet as He stayed awake just to admire her. How safe he felt holding her, how warm she made him even on the cool summer's night. Then, he fell asleep. In the morning, he woke to feel her beautiful mess of dark brown hair, suffocating him. He moved to breathe then started to admire the curves of her body that laid on him.

He never knew that he could feel so comfortable, vulnerable with another person. He thought that if he were wrong for thinking this was what true love felt like, he didn't want to be right. Just then she too woke up and glanced up from his chest.

"good morning," he said.

"you have bad breath," she smiled knowing how embarrassed that made him.

We don't know if these are the people we are meant to be with, whether they are *The One* or if they're teachers along our paths toward them. Not even the all-knowing narrator knows that. However, what all of us do know is that it is the little things that make love so special between two people. That night was just one of many memories they developed over many years of being the other's best friend.

Author's Note

Hilariously enough (to me), this was actually two different dates I had. One in high school and one in college.

I didn't want to just write about the date, but the lead up to the date because the preparation is just as important as the date itself. It is hilarious to me that no matter how much we plan and construct things to fall in line, nothing will go as planned. The first half, the dinner portion, was planned with the girl and of course I was rushed last minute. The second half, the beach, was another carefully constructed date night, only instead of eating at home, we got all the food we wanted, ate in the back of a car, and walked on the beach. This is purely one of those silly little stories that seemed to fit in the narrative of life and something most people would be able to relate to.

The major influence to write this silly story was Alexander Pushkin's short story, *The Shot*. That most of his stories were real stories or combinations of stories from his or other people's personal lives. For example in the shot, the duel came from his real life experience at dueling, most notably how the duelist approaches with a hat full of cherries that he is eating and spitting at the other duelist. This is something the mad lad did! Therefore this story is my attempt to copy his style of inspiration; the world around us.

EUGENE FYODR

(Part 1)

I

"There you are; you scoundrel!" She barks at me with a vicious growl.

I spring up from my project and meet her eyes, "Scoundrel?" I raise my eyebrows and my hand to my heart then pucker my lips "of what misdeed have I performed over you today?"

The young woman, made to be my wife, approached my workstation on the side of the house, "you are a scoundrel in all your fiber and being!"

"What could I have possibly done," I tease her, "speak you wretch."

"You!" Her stare could strike down any man and this excited me, "Eugene Fyoder!" Her voice cracks a little as all the air from her lungs leaves her as she emphasizes every other word, "Arrived home last night in the worst drunken state I have ever seen of man!"

"Oh what tragedy!" I cry out and fall, as though a fainting woman, to the end of her dress. "What sins I have!

How can you forgive me for spending an evening with ale and not cradled in your arms, my wife?" I stare into her eyes just as a puppy does once they have been caught next to their misdeeds.

"It is not that you were merely inebriated, Eugene!" She kicks me off her dress. "It is what you did and what I heard of your happening last night!" Her voice raises as if to suggest I have committed high treason.

I jump to my feet, "is there something my wife knows of what I have done, apart from sitting and singing the tavern songs of cheer and glee?"

"As a matter of fact I do!" She fires the last word like a bullet through my chest, "you!" She advances toward me.

"Me!" I mimic as I smile and turn this foot advance into a tango back walk.

"YOU!" Her face turns as red as a tomato ready to be picked from the field. "Only in such a super state, that you ran outside with Alexander and Ian to tip the neighbor's cow!"

She stops as I fall to the floor in a hysterical laugh. Caroline throws her hands on her hips and huffs.

"You scoundrel!" She reminds me. "You are lucky he thinks it was his own boy or he'd have your rear end to skin," her voice turns to pride, "and I would not hesitate to let him."

I stop laughing and raise myself to meet her eyes, "you would not dare …"

"Oh I would." She rises on her toes as an attempt to meet my height, meeting my eyes and begins to squint her own as though to pierce my soul. Oh, her face is stronger and more straight than any other I have met. She is strong, my Caroline, not like the soft, weak women of the village. No, my wife is hard as stone and as true as an archer's arrow.

The tension bubbles up as our faces inch closer in all sincerity. I cannot hold such a stance. Quickly and with great force, I give her a kiss on the lips and hug her.

"Let go of me!" Caroline is held in my tight grip, Caroline is held in my tight grip and laughs as she screams, "This is not funny! You are such a hooligan!" Her feet lift from the ground as I spin her in one big circle. I let her down on her feet and release her of my embrace.

She slaps my chest and exclaims, "you are a mad man, you know that! Any official would have half a mind to lock you up and throw away the key!"

"Ah, then is it a good thing that neither you nor I have half a brain to do such a thing." She gasps and starts in a full charge to me and I run into the hay pile to bring her down with me atop the hay. I wrap myself up to constrain her from doing any damage to myself. "Calm down, my wife, there is no need to be so aggressive." She stops and lays there in my arms on the hay.

"You will be the death of me Eugene, someday *woosh* I will be gone and you will have no one to set you on the right path."

"You know that it will be 10 years that we have been married in a few days, right Caroline?" We stare off into the distance, I can smell the lavender she uses to fragrant her hair. It is sublime to me.

"It will be." Her voice is soft and comforting, "we have been on this trail together for 10 years and no matter how crazy you drive me, I know you mean well."

I smile then kiss her head; I am too grateful to have such

a forgiving wife. "You do keep me on this right path, but my drunken adventures are not the worst to fall on us. An adventure it is, nothing more. Better yet, to stay here with you, wrapped in my embrace and captured by love."

Caroline grows a smile on her face, then sighed "And when I pass, you will walk away from the path we laid together, you will drink and adventure beyond your control. Only to depart from your rural kin to the city of pleasured sin. The path back will be longer than you would ever travel."

"Then let us hope I go before you." I calm down from my excitement, "can I find in you sympathy to allow me to tell you a selfish thought, wife?"

"Yes, husband?"

"I do hope I go before you though," I pause to hold my little treasure tighter in my arms, "I do not want to live a day without you there."

"Let us hope for both our sanity," She comforted me. "You better not drink that much tomorrow night. Only the good lord knows what you would do in the presence of my friends!"

I keep my eyes forward and bring my head closer to hers so that I can smell her hair, "of course not … you would interfere too often if I consumed that much!"

II

Silence is the sweet fragrance of my life. We lay in the hay for a long time, long enough for the sun to start his descent over the hill and set an orange blanket over the farm. Caroline's brown hair looks as though it were set on fire and her eyes are shut, painting the picture of my perfect wife. I get up and let her rest as the queen of her farm deserves.

"What harks have yet to been written in her glory will not be enough for the light she brings to my provincial kingdom." I say to my inner being. I leave the hay and make my way to the house.

I enter the house and see it is dark as night. The light from outside avoids me and retreats from the windows.

I stand by the water bucket on the table and wash my hands of the day's labor. "To ash we may return, but such filth we will be until then." I stare into the darkness absorbing the rooms and grin, "Darkness, you silent creature, why are people scared of you? Are you a monster? Do you hold monsters?" I walk to the other end of the room, "Or are you the bearer of secrets and we, as walking idiots, hide in your chest?"

Silence.

"Just as I thought, you are such a kind being." I stop to dry my hands, "but yet," I stare into the darkness, "for how kind and mysterious you are," I pause, "are you friend or foe?"

I ask the question to the darkness, and Darkness answers with a gentile, low, and reassuring voice, "no."

I sit at the table expecting the tax collector to emerge from one of the rooms, but nothing. I am growing concerned.

"From what depth have you come from?" No response. "Answer, you!" I accuse. "As you have done before!" Anger grips my words and fright caresses my body.

"From what depth have you emerged to enter my domain?" Darkness questions me as though I have infiltrated his home.

"No, no, no," I wave my finger at it, "you answer me, for you have entered *my* kingdom."

"Your kingdom lies within my domain and now you raise an issue with it." Darkness pauses briefly then emphasizes, "who … are … you?"

"I am Eugene Fyodr, king of my farm, earl to this building, and emperor to my destiny." I stand against Darkness. "You are Darkness, invader of lands, enemy of light, and now, foe to my eye."

"Enemy of light?" Darkness ponders, "Light is my mistress, I exist to please her work, I go where she cannot work to satisfy our empire."

"Then why do you run away if I were to light a candle?" I spark a lighter that I find on the table.

"For her, but for you I will extinguish it." Thus he destroys my flame to ember. "But just as a shadow is casted by the smallest of rocks in the meadow during a bright summer's day, just so light exists in the darkest of places." From the embers, a fire lights again and brightens my small corner of the room.

"You serve your queen with great fortitude." I pick up my pipe from the table and start to pack a conversational size of tobacco into it.

"It is the kingdom she desires, I cannot give her much, but that of which I can give, Eugene, is for her to know that she is needed. That I need her."

"You and I are not so different, Darkness." I light my pipe, then place the lighter down.

"How would you say?" Darkness engulfs the opposite end of the table. I continue to smoke.

"We both serve our strong wives, you in purpose and I

in our lives." The embers illuminate the inner workings of my pipe, yet I cannot see my hand.

"Is that what you do?" Darkness asks, "as humans, you live to appease others?"

"To me it is that way." I can only tell where I am from feel the finer end of the wood at the end of my mouth; the fact I sit on the chair; and after I puff, the smoke that rises from my mouth and into my nose.

Darkness laments, "I have only seen your kind slaughter each other. To harm one another in cruel makings of your own doings. You all have allow evils to seep into the core of your world."

"I am familiar with our works, yet at night you send howling beasts to stalk us at night," I accuse as I would with my friends, "You hide the truth beyond our vision, while during the day we are allowed to be free of those who would hurt us."

"My forgiving mistress gives you vision, but I take it away from you for a reason." Darkness's voice soothes the angst I have left in my body, I eagerly await his response, "The night beasts are to contain you, to tell you that you need your rest. They motivate you to remain in your dwellings until light can enter your homes, your fields, and your shops." Darkness pauses, "I fear what mankind can do if left to your own devices, the havoc and chaos you can bring upon the world my mistress is so affectionate towards."

"So you must contain us to protect us for her?" I suggest.

"Indeed, but you are not like the other humans I see." Darkness reassures me, "I have not seen a human be in similar service as I am in a very long time, my friend."

I finish my pipe, place it down, and yawn, "Indeed, you

are a great conversationalist, I hope our paths cross again my old friend."

"Our paths will, but until that day Eugene Fyodr." Then Darkness consumes everything.

※

In the dark I felt a jab on my side and Caroline voice pierces my ears, speaking incoherently. I open my eyes to reveal that it is day and I am on the floor beside the chair.

"Husband, breakfast is being prepared." She is soft in her speaking. The pipe sits properly on the table and the room is filled with cooking fat and eggs.

"What happened, wife?" I start to get up in the chair.

"I woke from my nap to discover you had left. I immediately thought to myself *what a scoundrel! He went off to drink with those damned boys again!* And of course I thought it strange when I entered the house and almost broke my neck over the lump of mass sprawled across the floor!" She points her finger to my place of slumber, " I thought you had snuck out, drank and ended up in a drunken slumber on the floor. I thought you would have learned a lesson if you spent a night on the floor, therefore left you."

"It is so nice to know I can find such solace in my wife during these troubling times," I throw my elbow on the table. My wife approaches me, cups her hands around my cheeks and bends over to make a face pouting into my own.

"Oh such tragedy that my drunken love cannot be trusted to not disappear into the night and reappear into the handle of a glass in the bars."

I lean slightly towards her and reply with great fluxion, "One day my princess, I am going to prove you wrong."

I start to wrap my hands around her, "then you will say *OH Eugene! What have I done to deserve such a man!*" She struggles against my hold, but fails as I pick her up and carry her around the table, "And there will be a great parade all in the name of the Fyodr husband and wife. There will be cheering, songs, and dance!" I take my wife, carry her in circles to simulate dancing and sing a tune to accommodate the setting.

III

When the work is minimal and the days are short, the bar is the only place to go to warm up without expending your own stockpile, as well as to have a cold brew. Caroline will frequently go to bed before me, therefore I frequent the tavern, along with the rest of the village, in an effort to be sociable during the shorter days.

"Eugene! come here, you are late!" Alexander calls me over. He is the definition of a man-child. His hair is short, but long enough to have a passing glance of curly quality to it. The way his face contorts, is more than any normal man's face. He would hear something shocking and his big bushy eyebrows would raise so high, you would believe me if I tell you that those bushy eyebrows would rise above his head. Even when they are relaxed, they seem to hide his eyes. Never in our friendship, have I ever seen his eyes. The corners of his mouth have a mind of their own as they move in different directions. Every time that boy looks at me, I have the strangest urge to take the closest pen and pad, draw the looks he gives, and treasure it forever as my personal heirloom to bring comedy for years to come.

"Eugene," Ian slurs, "you fiend!" Ian is an idiot who is like a tall idiot tree over the bar. There is nothing else about him worthy of note.

"Eugene, we were worried the time had come when we left the bar to find your body without its soul in the ditch outside," Alexander approached with a pitcher in hand.

"I hope my tardiness did not make you wish such horrors upon me," I bow as though I wait for an applaud, one I will never receive; I then bounce up, grab the pitcher and finish off the remaining liquid, skipping my taste buds and going directly down my guzzle.

"But that pitcher was for me …" Ian voice raises to be heard, but then dies as the last of his beer is drank. He lowers his head, "ok I will get another one." Ian slurs and stumbles his way to find the bar. When he is waist deep in inebriation, he is soft spoken and mumbles; I would expect it since he cannot have a conversation with anyone without squatting like a hen about to lay her egg.

"Eugene Fyodr, take this pitcher in the likes that you will become as terribly drunk … as terrible as you look." Alexander bellows out and hands me a new pitcher.

We clank our pitchers and swig, then place the empty container on the busy table. The waitress carries us new pitchers immediately, just as we raise the pitchers to toast to life.

"Eugene!" Ian professed. "We were talking of our younger days, specifically Alexander's inability to speak to women!"

"Damn you, Ian!" Alexander roars. "Do you wish the whole bar to know of our conversation?" He has a stern finger to his mouth and hissed at Ian.

Ian takes another sip of his drink, places it down, wipes his mouth of foam and states, "there is not much old Eugene can tell us that we do not already know. Most of his youth was preoccupied by Hannah until unforeseeable circumstances happened and led him to the drunken slob we see today!"

"A married, drunken slob," I remind Ian, " to someone who is figuratively my other half!"

"Who is Hannah?" Alexander asks in his regular ignorance.

"Does your mind leave you at every moment or just when you are awake, Alexander?" Ian smacks the shoulder of our friend, knowing full well the scar this memory has on my soul.

Ian looks to me for approval and I decide to ease the burden off of him, "Hannah is the woman who came before Caroline," I look around for anyone who could hear, "betwixt me, this story does." I look back into Alexander's eyes, "silence is important as this is the most sacred of any information I will divulge."

Alexander nods to agree and thus I begin.

"During the time before Caroline, when my father still taught me the meaning of work and my mother made my food, I worked the plot next to our family to help them as our neighbor had only Hannah to aid in household work. As the time passed on from year to year and we grew inch by inch, I grew a fondness to catch her eye. I would look for more work around their land just to catch a glimpse of her. Her father always accepted the help and I believe he knew as Hannah would always be there working outside the house when I would work."

Ian gulps down another pint and keeps it empty for the remainder of the story.

"On breaks I would spend it talking to her and tying my words in a way to sway her into my arms. And it worked, she was my first love as I was hers. She had the curliest brown hair that fell on her shoulders, her eyes had seen so many stars that they shined, and her voice was the nectar that bees look for all their lives. She could talk of the deepest of interest on the latest book she reads and how much more the world is beyond the eyes and the ears, but also in the heart and beyond our own minds."

I look deep into my cup; I try to read the ripples and bubbles under the light layer of foam as though I were a witch. "Every now and then I remember back to the day it ended. We were too hot headed and firm in our childish beliefs. I look back and remember I was too young to know what I do now. We both were. She could have made a gorgeous wife." I pause briefly to gather my words, "I did not know what I had until she was gone."

"Did you try to get her back? Did you ever see her?" Ian grasps his cup with both hands as Alexander sighs with great force.

"I moved over here to start my farm and Hannah disappeared from her childhood home." I take a moment just for myself. "When I met Caroline I was broken. She fixed me like a cobbler fixes our boots: one thread at a time. I owe a lot to her and I am the most fortunate man to have heaven and all its angels smile on me for her to be with me. Fortune has a mysterious path for all of us."

I get up, get another drink, then another, and another. Drink after drink, my eyes get hazy and blurry, then nothing.

✺

I wake to feel my head blistered as I rise in the dark abyss that surrounds me. *R.I.P. Henry Ripper* was the stone slab that met my eye upon my awakening.

"Well *this* is a great sign," I say to myself as I pick myself up and discover that I am in the middle of a sea of tombstones. I rub my forehead as I confirm that I am indeed with the dead in the night.

I rise and prop myself against the tombstone, "Mr. Ripper, I hope you would not mind that I rest here for a little." The light layer of fog on the ground remains undisturbed, of which I appreciate that I had not disturbed it when I rose. However, above the fog was the bleak blackness of night.

Out of the darkness a shadow emerges and props himself against the stone across from me, as though he is here for me. He had no features, since he was a shadow of nothing. As he draws closer I recognize his shape was that of a fat cat on his hind legs. He approaches, analyzing me with great concern, petting away at his whiskers.

"My host, do you have a drink?" I grin, but he remains silent and keeps making himself comfortable across from me, placing his paws to his sides. It is grossly difficult to tell but it seems like he is attempting to put his paws in his pockets or on his hips. This makes it difficult to tell me if he is relaxing or disappointed.

"You are not darkness, he would have had a drink." He remained silent.

"Frankly it does not matter," I put my grin back in my

42

pocket and stare off to the side of him; even squint off at the distant tree line that should be there in the darkness. "This is a lovely place, really; the silence, cool air, and fog which makes me believe they are soft to lay on." I look back at the oddly large, possibly fat, black cat. "A good place to retire to, when I am tired and aching." My host bows his head down, then slowly back up.

"To watch the sun set and rise, the wind and rain slowly erode my only marker on this mortal world," I take my hands out of my pocket and cross my arms. "Tell me my friend, did you have a good life?"

The fat, black cat made a trip around me to survey me as his model.

"Quite the life, do not rush to tell me at once," I cannot help but to give a small chuckle. "I like my life, be a shame if it went away." My host still says nothing, but returns across from me and sits as proper cats should upon tables, but here he sits on a tombstone.

"You are a very peculiar host," I try to peer deep into him, yet I cannot seem to find anything. "Is there nothing to you or is it that I am seeing you with the wrong eyes? How strange it is that I know you are here and yet, you are still so strange and mysterious; with humans it is easy, I simply ask or look at their features, but I cannot even see what is below the surface of your coat, let alone your skin. Does anyone?" My host lowers his head into his pawed cradle.

I lean back on Mr. Ripper's tombstone to take a quick glance at the night sky, "I feel like you wish to talk to me, but you cannot and I do not blame you, the cemetery is no place to have a lively talk with friends let alone a guest. As the ground might talk with the starry night, but cannot because of the fog." I look back at my host, "someone once wrote about how life's a walking shadow and compared such life as a stage performance, I do not remember much of it, but you seem the fellow who enjoys some research."

A dim light catches my eye through the fog, but still at a distance, "well sir, I appreciate your time." I support myself and stretch myself in preparation to walk, "but I guess I must be off now." I walk past my host, through the fog and toward the light.

Just then he looks up and with the deepest of voices to come echoing out from any living being's bowels, he speaks, "where are you going?"

I turn to see him with his eyes into the sun as he rises, "well, I'm going home. You were not one for conversation so I bid you farewell."

"Eugene Fyodr, you are as foolish as you are ignorant." The fat, black cat rises from the tombstone and onto his hind legs again, "neither wise nor smart." He starts to pet his whiskers again and approaches me, he studies me, "yet you still manage to wife the neighbor's daughter, stay with your life friends, all while withering your life away one drink at a time."

I am off put, "I know I may not be the smartest rock in the field, but I do have my wife whom I love with the deepest parts of my soul and my friends-" the cat interrupts.

"Friends?" The fat, black cat giggles, "you live your small life, in your small house, with your small people." He pulls the grass from the roots and studies them, "they are all as things just like this grass is a thing to me," he drops them, "things; but I, Eugene, I am big."

"Pray do tell." He captures my curiosity to see the extent by which this cat can go on.

"You live your life on this narrow path, set to you by these friends, your wife, your parents, your church, and your state." The cat commences to walk in circles around me, "abiding by the repetitive rules you restrict yourself to religiously and rigorously follow," he stops in front of me, "but you, my dear Eugene, I come feeling generous today." He jumps on a tombstone behind him and sits with his legs hanging off.

"You had my curiosity, but now you have my attention. Why generous today? Of all days?"

"I shall start with my lunch." How odd to start in the middle, but not the worst place to start, better than starting at the end, I'd say.

The cat began, "several years ago I was just a small cat sitting on the window sill of my owner's apartment in New York City, when a sharply dressed man offered my owner a once in a lifetime opportunity to change his life if he would be so kind as to join him." The cat shakes his head as though to say no, "alas my owner refused, and at once turned to me and asked if I desired a change." He gestures up and down at himself, "and thus he gave this feline the ability to talk, walk, dance, and sing." He presses on, "I had great fun with my new master." He looks off into the distance, "visiting Moscow, Paris, Casablanca, and Tokyo." He looks to the other side, "Siane, Sudan, Syria, and Southern Canada." He abruptly explains, "not northern, no use for a fat feline north of Nova Scotia." He returns to his passage, "And upon returning from Copenhagen and Osla, I decided to see what the poor provincial people were going on about, and became drastically bored, then I happened upon you wondering in the morning fog." He shrugs at his shoulders, "so I think to myself, why not entertain myself." The fat black cat turns his gaze into mine, " I know why you are so different from everyone else."

"A cat wandering the world?" I ask grossly, "what do you do? Do you work? Are you a knave? A vagabond?"

The fat cat laughs to himself, "Neither, I am a businessman and my employer looks for people just like you to employ for his business."

"And what business is that?"

"None of yours if you keep asking all these questions." The cat continues on his story as though nothing has happened, "So I start to write my employer about you and as I am writing I think to myself, why write about it, why not just show the poor soul." now that cat holds out his hand as to make a deal, "so I ask you, Eugene Fyodr, would you be so kind as to join me on a once in a lifetime opportunity."

"But my wife? What of my land and animals?" I ask the obvious questions, "How are they to-"

The cat interrupts again, "need not worry about such trivial things, the employer will settle any differences. Just as my old owner has a cat, your wife shall have a new income."

Part of me says no, yet the other half tells me to take the dive of adventure, "say I do not want to do this after meeting your employer, will I return in a timely fashion?"

"Oh I will deliver you to the threshold of your door if you so decide to, but I must warn you, not many people return from the employer's office with the desire to come back home."

I shake the cat's fat paw and *woosh*, we vanish from the graveyard.

IV

The cat and I appear at the entrance of a great office, one I have never seen before. There is more than enough room to fit two bars into and still have room for Caroline and myself to live in. The floor to ceiling windows let in the bronze light from outside. The cat goes over to the wooden double doors, which stretch from the ground and into the ceiling which seems to be over thrice my own height. He opens one door, "come on, he will see us now."

I follow and catch the door as the cat releases it. My lord, I almost lose wind and my own mortal being with how heavy this thing is, made of a thousand stone bricks I think. There is one man sitting behind a small table, built to the length of my height and as tall as my dining room table, yet only enough space on top as to seem the employer is the only space allowed on it. The bronze light makes him out to be tanner than I assume he is, considering he looks as though he has been at that desk for five years or more with no food or water.

"Woland, I have-." The cat is interrupted by the employer's work and his eyes gaze up toward mine.

"Good afternoon, my dear Eugene Fyodr!" As an apple attracts to the ground, my eyes are drawn to his red pupils. "Please allow me to introduce myself," and with a swing of his arm, a small dish of caviar appears at the end of his desk in front of the chair he expects me to sit in, "I'm a man of wealth and taste." The way he speaks is something I have never heard before, it was as though he speaks my language but his mouth and tongue move in different ways.

I approach the chair and sit, "fascinating display of magic." I accept the caviar, but I do not eat it, "but I must profess that I do not have an acquired taste for fish."

The fat, black cat walks over to the desk next to me, "then may I?" he asks as he directs his paw toward the caviar to which I gesture to say of course.

Woland seems to study my actions then he speaks, "What is your taste then, Eugene Fyodr?"

"I must profess to you that I do not have many wishes," I ponder about what I enjoy in the world.

"My dear Eugene Fyodr," a peculiar smiles draws across Woland's face, "anything valuable in the world and it can be a wish."

"Beer" is the first word that comes to mind.

"If beer is all you desire," Woland's peculiar grin began to startle my stomach, "then we can accommodate." Then in the place where the caviar had previously been, a pint of beer appeared.

I grab the cool glass and bring the lip to mine to smell the best beer I have ever drank, "tell me mister-?"

"Woland," he states.

"Woland," I sip on the beer, "what do you do?"

"Of all the questions you have and you ask what I do?" Woland is perplexed.

"Well I already know I'm in a dream, where else can beer appear out of thin air and a fat, black cat walks on two legs?" I anticipate to wake up at any moment.

"Ahh you think you're dreaming, very well," His grin

turns to oblivious amusement, "then I am a professor of black arts,"

"Interesting, and what brings you to my small world, Woland?" I rise from the chair and move to the white windows, which becomes more apparent that it is simply a soft white cloth.

"Your small world is merely part of my larger world." Woland remains seated. I approach the window and peak behind to reveal a wondrous town with many buildings, the amount I have never seen in my life, with colorful onion shaped domes vibrant with red, blue, gold, and green.

Before I can open my mouth, a pale man with an astonishingly long red beard rushes to Woland's desk. "Woland, Woland!" He cries.

"John George, may I introduce you to-" Woland is interrupted.

"Woland it is looking very bad, I cannot put my finger on it, but I-I-I-I-I" John George incoherently stumbles through the rest of his sentence. I fail to understand why this skinny, elegantly dressed man, with his thick long red beard would have anything to worry about. I imagine he would be able to pay for others to worry for him, but no.

"John George!" Woland cheerfully cried, he rose from his desk and went around to meet John George. "now calm down and simply tell me what is the matter." Woland held John Goerge's hands and cupped them together. John George's gaze shoots in my direction which causes me to feel for the safety of the wall. His red and beady eyes are more horrifying than when Caroline tries to strike me down with her gaze when she is angry. "It is safe my friend, he is a new employee! John George this is-"

John George continues to stare at me and calmly interrupts, "Mars comes closest tonight than in all previous years during a full moon!" John George looks back at Woland, who stares without expression at John George.

There is a brief uncomfortable silence in the conversation, I can still hear the fat black cat's caviar spoon hit his teeth from the corner of the room, "Well this is good, no?" Woland comes back to life, his voice as energetic as before, "You remember the last time we performed during a full moon?"

"It was a resounding success," John George finally calms down, "a little crazier than our normal ones," his voice rises, "but nothing you could not handle."

"See?" Woland exclaims.

"But Mars is closer to Earth now than it has ever been!" John George raises his voice again only to be met with Woland's soothing voice.

"now, now," Woland is the most calm I have seen him yet, it is almost erie, "you have nothing to worry about during the performance by old friend, because you will be here counting our finances," Woland points to his desk, "it will be our problem to deal with *them*" Woland's emphasis on that word disgusts me.

"I guess you are right." A sign of relief and serenity comes over John George, "I will still be protected, right? He inquires, Woland nods his head

"Then we have nothing to fear, my friend!" Woland puts his arm around John Goerge's shoulders and guides him toward the entrance, but on their third step together, Woland grabs the back of John George's neck to pull his ear to Woland's mouth., "and if you ever," Woland's tone causes the fat black cats scatters from his food to hide under the desk. I am astonished how hateful his voice can become. His volume rises as he nears the end of his thought, until he is screaming, "dare to interrupt me as I am speaking to you again!"

The door slams shut after Woland pushes John George out the door. The fat black cat reappears and walks back to his caviar. Woland exhals, "my dearest apologies Eugene Fyodr," he rushes to his desk where a paper on the corner of his desk has caught fire. Woland takes his arm and extinguishes it as though it were more of a nuisance than anything else, "some people can be so rude sometimes, do not mind him. I gaze back at the large white buildings which span beyond the horizon. Woland speaks up, "I have a use for you in my next appearance, I plan to host tonight."

"And what would you have me do?" Something about this dream filled me with a sense of wonder, the likes of which I have not felt in a long time. Surly this is an amazing display of the things the mind can dream.

"Behemoth," Woland calls and the big, fat, black cat directs his attention from the corner, "show Eugene Fyodr to the spare room so he may prepare for tonight. As for you my curious friend, all I need you to do is show up."

Then the fat, black cat guides me to the room we entered from as the waiting area has turned into a small bedroom with a beautiful white sink in the corner. "Dear host, is there any-" and the door closed behind me, the fat, black cat is gone and I am left alone to discover the room.

-End of Part 1 -

Author's Note

Eugene Fyodr is my first attempt at building a full narrative. I was inspired after seeing a production of *Peer Gynt* by Norwegian Playwright Henrik Ibsen to write a three part vignette titled *The Wife, The Darkness, and The Friend* in 2017. It stayed like that until I came back to revise and edit the story and realized that there is more to be explored in Eugene's world and exercise my ability to world build in writing under the narration of Eugene Fyodr and his adventure "off the path". This was around the same time I was rereading *The Master and Margarita* by Mikhail Bulgakhov and decided to include the characters of Woland and Behemoth for the fanciful world Eugene Fyodr lives in. The intention to include those characters is for people who have read Bulgakhov's work to give those attentive readers a little Easter Egg and an idea of the fun and crazy things I'm planning for part 2 which at the time of publication is still under development.

I knew this is something I definitely wanted to revise when I sent the rough draft to my housemate, Kim, for notes. I definitely have to thank her for being the first to read the rough first draft and provide feedback that really helped to bring Eugene to life as a character from my mind and onto the page.

It has been interesting to see how coming back to old stories can inspire a change in them. Originally Behemoth was a shadow man, almost a ghost, who didn't speak and guided Eugene to death, but reflecting back I realize Eugene didn't need to die for the story and that it was dramatic for no reason with no resolution. As I grow as a writer, I have begun to exercise important questions about my stories, "what is the story trying to tell? How do I get there? And are the characters doing what they need to do that will result in a satisfying resolution?" Writing has always been an adventure in itself. I can only hope that reading these will be as satisfying to the reader as it was, writing them, for me.

Printed in the United States
By Bookmasters